NORMAN
the Lion

by Laura Gates Galvin

Illustrated by Christopher Leeper

AFRICAN WILDLIFE FOUNDATION®

KIDS!

To my loving husband John, without whom I would not be complete — L.G.G.

To my family for their love and support — C.L.

Book copyright © 2003 Trudy Corporation

Published by Soundprints division of Trudy Corporation, Norwalk, Connecticut

Book design: Marcin D. Pilchowski
Book layout: Jennifer Kinon
Editor: Chelsea Shriver

First Edition 2003
10 9 8 7 6 5 4 3 2 1
Printed in China

Acknowledgments:
   Our very special thanks to Elodie Sampéré at AWF for all her graceful assistance, Henry Kankomba Mwima, wildlife expert, and all the staff at the African Wildlife Foundation.

Library of Congress Cataloging-in-Publication Data

Galvin, Laura Gates, 1963-
   Norman the lion / by Laura Gates Galvin ; illustrated by Christopher J. Leeper.
      p. cm.
   Summary: Norman, a young lion who lives alone, uses a lot of energy trying to find something to eat.
   ISBN 1-59249-189-8 – ISBN 1-59249-190-1 (pbk.)
   1. Lions--Juvenile fiction. [1. Lions--Fiction.] Leeper, Christopher J., 1966- ill. II Title.

PZ10.3.G153No 2003
[E]—dc21
                                                                                 2003050362

NORMAN
the Lion

by Laura Gates Galvin
Illustrated by Christopher Leeper

Soundprints
Where Children Discover...

A hot day slowly comes to an end as the brilliant sun begins to set in Zambia, Africa. A young lion stretches and yawns after a short nap in the shade.

Along the river, groups of animals journey together. But Norman is a young lion. He is alone. He used to live with his family in a pride. Now he is five years old and it is time for him to live on his own for a short while.

Norman slowly gets to his feet. He is hungry and thirsty after his sleep. He walks to the river's edge and laps up the cool water. As Norman drinks, something catches his eye. He quietly lifts his head to get a closer look.

Norman sees a dark green shape floating in the water. Could this be food? A single log floats in the river near him. Norman carefully puts his front paws onto the log so he can peer over it and get a closer look at the shape in the water.

It's a tortoise! The tortoise will make a tasty snack for Norman. He leans over the log, and bats at the tortoise with his front paw, but he can't quite reach it. He carefully pulls himself onto the log.

The log begins to wobble and shake as Norman tries to keep his balance. Then the log and Norman slowly drift away, farther and farther from the shore.

Norman quickly forgets the tortoise —
he wants to be back on land, not in the water!
Norman and the log begin to circle and
slowly float in the direction of the shore.

Splash! Norman leaps into the shallow water. He runs from the shore, stopping under an acacia tree. He plops down with a yawn and rolls in the shade.

Norman is even hungrier after his water adventure. He hasn't eaten anything in days. He sees something moving in a nearby bush. He quietly sneaks over to see what it is.

Norman sticks his nose in the bush to get a better look. It's a lizard! Norman traps the lizard with his giant paw. But suddenly Norman sees the lizard running away. He has only caught the lizard's tail!

Norman runs after the lizard. The lizard is fast, but not as fast as Norman! At last, Norman catches some food.

Norman spends the early evening looking for more food. He chases a wildebeest, but he can't catch it. He chases a zebra, but it also gets away.

Norman is very tired from all his effort. As the moon lights up the night sky, Norman gives himself a bath. Later tonight Norman will hunt for more food, but for now, he will settle down for a much needed nap.

AFRICAN WILDLIFE FOUNDATION® KIDS!

Would you like to learn more about Norman and other lions and animals in Africa?

Soundprints and the African Wildlife Foundation invite you to visit our website and sign up for monthly e-mail updates about Norman and other African lions.

Log on to:
www.awf.org/norman/

PRIVACY NOTE: Soundprints and the African Wildlife Foundation want to assure all participants who sign up for monthly updates on these fascinating animals that their e-mail address will be kept confidential and will be used for the sole purpose of sending these requested monthly updates from Soundprints and the African Wildlife Foundation. Under no circumstances will any information collected specifically for these e-mail updates be sold or distributed to any other organization for any other purpose.

Soundprints
Where Children Discover...

AFRICAN WILDLIFE FOUNDATION® KIDS!

ABOUT THE AFRICAN WILDLIFE FOUNDATION

For more than 40 years, the African Wildlife Foundation (AWF) has played a major role in ensuring the continued existence of some of Africa's most rare and treasured species. AWF has invested training and resources in African individuals and institutions that have played critical roles in conservation. The essential need to conserve Africa's remaining vital ecosystems inspired AWF to mark a new era in African conservation by establishing the African Heartlands Program. AWF Heartlands are large, cohesive land areas where governments, organizations, and individuals focus their joint conservation efforts. Ecologically, the Heartlands provide ample habitat for viable populations of wildlife to live, search for food and reproduce naturally. Economically, the Heartlands are increasingly valuable assets as wilderness becomes rare in our world. These wildlife attractions draw investors and offer enterprise opportunities that improve local economies and create wealth.

The African Wildlife Foundation, together with the people of Africa, works to ensure that the wildlife and wild lands of Africa will endure forever.

About Henry Kankomba Mwima, Wildlife Expert

Henry Mwima is a native of Zambia, southern Africa, and has had an extensive career in wildlife as a ranger, biologist and wildlife research officer. He holds a BS in wildlife biology from North Carolina University and a MS in Rural and Land Ecology from the International Institute for Aerospace Survey and Earth Sciences in the Netherlands.

He has been working as a heartland coordinator for the AWF for the past three years and he is responsible for promoting landscape level conservation in the Four Corners Trans-boundary Natural Resources Management Area covering Botswana, Namibia, Zambia, and Zimbabwe.

Henry resides in Zambia, Africa, with his wife and two children.

About African Lions

Lions live mostly in Africa and are part of the cat family. They are very big cats!

Male lions can weigh up to 550 pounds and female lions can weigh up to 350 pounds!

Lions live throughout the Sahara desert and are found in grassy plains, savannahs, open woodlands and scrub country. They live in family groups called prides. Prides are made up of several females, a few young cubs and one or two male lions. Young male lions like Norman leave the pride when they are five years old. They live on their own for approximately the next three years before joining another pride. Nicknamed King of the Jungle, the lion is a beautiful and strong creature.